The Window Wonders

Story by Michael Pryor

Illustrations by Scott Brown

Contents

Chapter 1	Shattered	5
Chapter 2	Dollars Down the Drain	10
Chapter 3	Beware of the Dogs	13
Chapter 4	Run Away!	18
Chapter 5	Lords of the Lawn	25
Chapter 6	Refreshment Royalty	32
Chapter 7	Sales Success!	39
Chapter 8	The Music Masters	43
Chapter 9	Tough Competition	47
Chapter 10	It Made a Great Story	54

Chapter 1

Shattered

Kai is my best friend. We live in the same neighbourhood, and even though we grew up together, he still surprises me with some of his wild ideas.

We were over at his place one day, doing homework together, when he looked up and pointed his pen at me. "Hey, Vikram. Do you know how to make a basketball bounce really, really high?"

When Kai asks a wacky question like that, a million answers race around inside my head. "Well," I said, "you could get on a rocket, go up to the International Space Station and drop it from there. That'd work."

Kai got a faraway look in his eyes. "That's not a bad idea." He shook his head. "But I meant right now."

I sighed. "I give up. How do you make a basketball bounce really, really high?"

Kai dropped his pen on the table and closed his maths book. "Wait here," he said, "and come outside when you hear my whistle."

"I guess you want me to finish the rest of the maths problems while I wait," I said.

Kai gave me a fist bump. "And that's why we're best friends, Vikram."

I got on with the problems, which was easier without Kai. He has a few annoying habits when he's bored, and he gets bored easily when he's doing homework. For instance, he taps his pen on the table in front of him. *Tap, tap, tappity tap.* Over and over and over again. He doesn't even realise he's doing it.

I had just finished the last problem and was stretching my arms over my head when I heard Kai's whistle. He's a good whistler. If he really got going, I reckon you could hear him on the other side of the country.

I wandered out the back. Kai has a nice backyard with plenty of lawn and garden and some big trees. There's even a birdbath, because his mum likes seeing birds having a good splashy wash.

Kai was on the concrete area in front of the garage, next to a ladder. He had a basketball in his hands, and he was grinning. "I bet this is science, or something," he said.

Straightaway, I saw what Kai was planning. "If you try to bounce the basketball from the top of that ladder, it's going to go on the roof of the garage." I pointed. "Or get caught in that tree, and you'll never get it down."

Kai grinned. "This is another reason why we're a good team. I dream the dream, while you pay attention to the details."

"Here," I said, and I dragged the ladder closer to the birdbath. "You'll be better off if this thing is facing the other direction."

"Got it."

Kai climbed right to the top of the ladder. He wasn't really watching where he put his feet, so I steadied it. After all, I had seen plenty of Kai's disasters in the past. I'm not saying that Kai is accident-prone, but he once got his finger stuck in a drain just because he wanted to see if he could touch the water at the bottom. The fire brigade had to come and help get his hand free.

"Are you ready?" Kai asked, looking down at me.

"You know what?" I replied. "I'd be a lot happier if you'd hang on to the ladder with one hand."

"I'm fine," he said. "I reckon I could be a tightrope walker because my sense of balance is so good."

Did I tell you that Kai has a lot of confidence in himself?

"Okay," he said. "One, two, THREE!"

Kai heaved with both hands and threw the basketball up as high as he could. It shot into the air like a rocket. At the top of its climb, it slowed and paused. Then it began to drop back down to earth, faster and faster, until it landed on the concrete path with a satisfying *SMACK!*

Kai was right. It did bounce really, really high, but it went a little crookedly. After it had gone up really, really high, it came down again. But instead of landing on the concrete, it hit the edge of the birdbath. While Kai and I stared, the basketball shot off at an angle, right through the big kitchen window. Glass shattered with a horrible crunching noise that sounded like very expensive trouble.

Kai turned to me. "I can honestly say that I didn't expect that to happen."

Chapter 2

Dollars Down the Drain

I offered to go inside with Kai, because it was partly my fault, after all. I'd moved the ladder, hadn't I? Kai shook his head. "It was my stupid idea," he said. "I guess I'll face the music."

He trudged through the front door. His head was down and his shoulders were slumped. I packed up the ladder and leant it against the garage.

Kai came out some time later. His shoulders were even more saggy. "I have to pay to get the window fixed," he said.

"How much will it be?"

Kai told me and I nearly fell over. "That's a fortune!" I said. "It's going to take you forever to pay it off!"

"It was a big window." Kai sighed. "Lots of glass. That means no spending money for me for a long, long time. Goodbye, chocolate bars. Farewell, comic books."

I punched him lightly on the shoulder. "We'll go halves. It was partly my fault."

Kai shook his head. "Thanks, but no thanks. I have to take the blame. After all, it was my last chance."

I slapped my forehead. "I'd forgotten about that."

Kai had been on his last chance for some time. After all, just this year there had been the accident with the paint, the broken door handle and the Great Laundry Flood. His parents must have decided his chances had finally run out.

Kai's face fell. "And it means no Hawaiian shirt, either, not until forever."

This got him where it hurt. He'd been saving up for a really colourful Hawaiian shirt he'd seen. It was blue with huge pink hibiscus flowers on it, and I thought it was so loud it could be seen from the moon, but he thought it was stylish. It would certainly make him stand out.

It was time for a pep talk. "What if we could come up with a way to pay off your debt quicker?" I asked.

He frowned. "What do you mean?"

"You're Kai, right? The one who has a hundred ideas and a thousand plans?"

"True. Nothing to argue with there."

"Snap out of it, then! Don't get sad, get thinking."

Kai lifted his head. He gazed at the sky. "I can do that."

"If anyone can, you can."

"That's right. All I need are a few good schemes to make some money. I'll pay for the window, and that Hawaiian shirt will be mine before we know it!"

I slapped him on the back. "That's the spirit! Where are we going to start?"

Kai grinned. "Well, I've got this idea."

Chapter 3

Beware of the Dogs

The next day, I carried the buckets and Kai carried the ladder. "You see," he said to me. "The ladder got me thinking."

"And the window," I said.

"Well, yes, the window. Not *breaking* glass, though. Cleaning it."

This was Kai's Big Idea. We'd go up and down our street and clean windows to earn some cash. Simple, easy, no problem, right? He even had a name for us.

"We can call ourselves the Window Wonders," he said. "And we can get caps with a *WW* emblem, and t-shirts, and special buckets with *WW* on them, and business cards and stuff like that."

"One step at a time," I said, because Kai often let his imagination run away with him. "Are you sure your parents are okay with this?"

Kai waved a hand. "They're totally happy any time I have a good idea like this."

"Are you sure?" I asked, cautiously.

"Sure I'm sure. We know everyone in the street, and I bet they'll be glad to have their windows cleaned. It's our ticket to fabulous riches!"

"Calm down, calm down," I said, making soothing gestures. "Let's try a few window-cleaning jobs first and see how it goes."

We sized up the houses in our street and decided that the Lee family's house would be a good one to try first. It had lots of windows, and the garden was neat and tidy. We both agreed that overgrown gardens would be trouble for window cleaning, especially if they had thorny bushes. I didn't want to go fighting through dense undergrowth like a jungle explorer.

Mr Lee answered the door when we knocked. He was happy for us to clean his windows, and we were happy with what he offered to pay us. He told us to be careful of his dogs, though. They got excited around strangers.

Kai waved a hand. "No problem. Dogs love us, don't they, Vikram?"

Kai had no idea about dogs, really, but he *thought* he did. Any dogs we met, he'd call them "good doggie" or "attaboy". He'd woof at them and insist that he was speaking their language, even when they seemed to roll their eyes at him.

"We'll be fine," I said to Mr Lee.

We started with the easy-to-reach parts of the windows. With lots of water and a good scrubbing action with sponges, the windows started to gleam.

Kai whistled while he worked. I think he was counting his money already.

For safety's sake, I made sure that I was the one who went up the ladder. Kai held it, and I cleaned the top parts of the windows with my sponge. I made sure to get right into the corners, because if a job is worth doing, it's worth doing properly, right?

When we finished the front windows, we stood back and admired our work. The windows were crystal clear and the sun glistened on them. "That is some top-class window cleaning," Kai said, his hands on his hips. "They look as good as new."

I squeezed the water out of my shirtsleeve. We'd only got a little bit wet, really. Kai was enthusiastic with his sponge, and I got splashed plenty of times from his energetic cleaning.

"Down the side and around the back?" I suggested.

We went around the side of the house with our buckets, sponges and ladder. I groaned. Five big windows waited for us – and then there was the back of the house and the other side.

Kai shrugged. "I guess we should have counted the windows before we agreed on a price."

It took us some time to finish the side windows, and by then I was dripping wet, as was Kai. Good thing it was a warm day.

We reached the gate that led to the back of the house. It had a sign on it, saying, "Beware of the Dogs". Another sign underneath said, "Muffin and Puffin are at home".

Kai laughed. "Muffin and Puffin? They sound cute!"

True enough. Dogs who were named things like "Killer" or "Brutus" were usually giant-sized with big, sharp teeth. Muffin and Puffin? Fluffballs, probably.

I peered over the fence and saw a nice garden, with some flower beds and a fish pond next to a small in-ground trampoline. A very small dog kennel was near the back door of the house. It had "Muffin and Puffin" written on the roof.

"If they fit in that kennel," I said, "they can't be very big."

Kai opened the gate. "Tiny and cute. My favourite kind of dogs."

Chapter 4

Run Away!

Getting the ladder and the buckets through the gate was tricky, but we finally made it. I propped the ladder up against the house while Kai counted the windows. “Six plus a big double one,” he said. “You know, we really need to improve our quoting.”

I started getting the ladder ready while Kai went to the tap to fill the buckets. He whistled happily as he went. I think he was seeing himself in his new Hawaiian shirt already.

Kai carried the buckets back. He was still whistling, but he stopped short when an angry bark came from the dog kennel.

“I think you’ve woken Muffin,” I said to Kai. “Or it might be Puffin.”

Kai turned around. “I’m sorry, Muffin!” he called. “Don’t worry, Puffin. The Window Wonders are friendly!”

A dog came out of the kennel. At least, it could have been a dog. It looked more like a snowball with two black eyes and a little black nose. It was about the same size as a large grapefruit, and it took one look at us and barked. "Muffin?" asked Kai.

Another dog came out of the kennel. It looked the same as the other one, but its nose was pink. So cute!

Then one of them growled. It sounded as if it had been woken up from a very good sleep and it definitely wasn't happy. The other one joined in and did some pretty good teeth gnashing too.

"I don't think Puffin liked your whistling," I said to Kai. "Or was it Muffin?"

"That's a shame," he said. More growling. Kai crouched and held out his hand. "Come on, doggos, let's be friends."

One of them wiggled a little, then charged. The other howled and raced after it. I'd never seen dogs move so fast. They were like bolts of snowball-sized lightning. They raced at the crouching Kai and sprang, knocking him into a backwards somersault. "Waargh!" cried Kai as he collided with one of the buckets. Water went everywhere, mostly on Kai.

I didn't have time to worry about Kai drowning because the next thing they turned on was me. I quickly opened the ladder and raced up it, away from the furry terrors – just in time.

Yapping, the dogs leapt up and barely missed my foot. One grabbed my shoelace and almost dragged me off the steps. Luckily, it tried to bark at the same time, and I whipped my foot free.

Kai sat up. "Muffin! Puffin!" he yelped. "I thought we could be friends!"

One of the dogs turned its head and snarled. The other one joined in. Together, they pounced on Kai's shoelace. They snapped their heads from side to side, and in an instant, they had dragged Kai's shoe off his foot.

"Hey!" Kai cried, but it was too late. They were off, racing around the backyard with Kai's shoe. Muffin had one shoelace, and Puffin had the other. The shoe dangled in between them as they tore around the garden.

They reached the back fence. Without slowing, they turned and headed back towards Kai. “Hey!” he cried, as Muffin and Puffin raced at him, holding on tight to the shoelaces. They were going to go either side of him, and Kai would get a nasty boot in the face!

Kai jumped to his feet, and in a split second he was perched on top of the ladder with me.

The dogs circled below in a growling blur.

“You’re not afraid of them, are you?” I asked Kai. The ladder wobbled a little.

“Any sensible person would be,” he pointed out. “They’re terrors.”

Muffin and Puffin stopped their circling. They didn’t let go of Kai’s shoe, though. They looked up at us, then they backed off. They went all the way to the back fence. They put their snouts down and their bottoms up. They wiggled. They charged. Right at the ladder.

Kai looked at me. I looked at him. “There’s only one thing we can do,” he said.

I nodded. We jumped.

“Waaargh!” Kai and I screamed as the ladder was swept away from underneath us, just after we jumped. “Whoaaa!” we howled as we landed on the in-ground trampoline.

Sproing! we went as we flew into the air.

I landed safely on the grass, surprising myself at how I managed it. Then Kai landed, but he was more unsteady. He was right on the edge of the fish pond, and his arms flailed as he tried to keep his balance. "No, no, no, no!" he wailed as he lost it. Just as he fell, one flailing hand grabbed my arm and pulled me down with him.

"Wurggle!" we spluttered as we landed in the fish pond with a huge splash.

Muffin and Puffin waddled up to the edge of the pond. They dropped Kai's shoe in, went back to their kennel and disappeared inside.

The fish pond wasn't very deep, but it was a bit green and grungy. Kai wiped water from his face. "There has to be a better way to make money than this," he said.

Chapter 5

Lords of the Lawn

"This one's a sure-fire winner," Kai said to me, as he held up a poster he'd printed.

Lords of the Lawn! Lawns mown cheap!

Expert service! (Sorry, no dogs.)

"We're Lords of the Lawn now? Not the Window Wonders?" I asked him.

"We change with the times, just like our teachers say businesses need to," he said. "We're modern and fast-moving like that."

I frowned. "Maybe you haven't considered everything. Are we even allowed to use a lawnmower, for instance?"

Kai grinned. "And that's where this isn't just a Big Idea, it's a Great Idea. We're not going to use a lawnmower."

"What are we going to use? Scissors?"

Kai looked like he was going to burst. "I have an aunty with a goat."

That afternoon, we stood outside Kai's place, and while we waited for his Aunty Roula, Kai explained. "Aunty Roula has lots of goats on her goat farm. She said she'll pay me to look after Clarence for her."

I took a guess. "Clarence is one of her goats."

"Right. So it's like double the money." Kai was so excited, he was waving his arms around. "We let Clarence eat the grass, and we get paid. We mind Clarence, and we get paid. It's perfect!"

I scratched my chin. "Have you ever looked after a goat before?"

"Not really."

"Not really?"

"Not at all, I suppose." Kai grinned. "But it's easy. Aunty Roula says that Clarence is her favourite because he's very easy-going."

As usual, I was already thinking of things that could go wrong. Kai saw it in my face. He punched me on the shoulder gently. "Don't be such a worrywart, Vikram! This is sure to be a success!"

Kai's Aunty Roula drove up in a big red truck. In the back was a goat. I guessed it was Clarence.

Aunty Roula was tall and wore blue overalls. She had dark eyes, lots of rings on her fingers and curly dark hair.

RM GRL

"Kai!" she cried when she climbed out of the truck. "And is this your friend Vikram?"

She grabbed my hand and shook it.

"Tell me about the time you saved Kai when he got tangled in that tennis net!" said Aunty Roula.

"He told you about that?"

"He did. And about the time you dragged him out after he fell into that compost bin. And about the time you wouldn't let him have that fourteenth piece of watermelon, which was probably a very good idea."

I looked at Kai again. He shrugged. "I tell Aunty Roula lots of things."

Aunty Roula helped Clarence down the ramp and gave Kai the rope that Clarence had around his neck. "Now, remember, Clarence is a very sensitive goat."

Kai nodded. "I'll remember."

"And he's my favourite, which is why I'm letting you take care of him while your uncle and I paint his goat shed."

"We'll take extra good care," Kai promised.

Aunty Roula patted Clarence on the head. Clarence bleated and rubbed up against her leg. "I usually like to take him for a walk in the morning," Aunty Roula added, "but I haven't had time today, so be kind to him." She patted Clarence on the head again. "Be good, Clarence," she told him.

Aunty Roula jumped back in the truck and drove off.

Clarence was a big white goat with big horns and a funny little chin beard. He looked at us. Then he looked at Aunty Roula's truck as it trundled away. He looked at us again, and he wasn't impressed. He bleated. He looked towards Aunty Roula's truck again, then shook his mighty head. With a heave, he tugged the rope out of Kai's grasp and galloped after the truck.

Kai's mouth dropped open. "That wasn't supposed to happen." He waved his hands over his head. "Come back, Clarence!"

And that's how we spent the rest of the day chasing a goat, instead of making money mowing lawns.

Eventually, we tracked Clarence down to the local park, where he was eating some bushes and looking around sadly for Aunty Roula. We tried to drag him back to Kai's place so he could eat the lawn, as a trial, but he wasn't keen. He planted all four hooves on the ground and wouldn't budge. When he put his head down and shook those horns at us, we both slowly backed away.

"I wonder if your Aunty Roula told Clarence about this arrangement," I said to Kai. "He doesn't seem to be very interested in it."

Kai sighed and rang his Aunty Roula.

An hour later, the big red truck rumbled up and took an overjoyed Clarence away.

We sat on the kerb and waved.

"So that's the end of Lords of the Lawn?" I asked Kai.

"I guess so," he said. "It's probably a good thing in the end. I could feel my hay fever starting to play up."

Kai was looking dejected again, so I nudged him with my elbow. "So what's next?"

"Next?" he said.

"Haven't you heard? My friend Kai never runs out of ideas. I just have to wait around for the next brilliant scheme to come along."

Kai brightened. "That's right. Giving up isn't the way to success! The next big thing is the way to success!"

"And what is it?" I asked.

Kai blinked, then a slow smile spread across his face. "I think you're going to like this one."

Chapter 6

Refreshment Royalty

Two days later, Kai and I were in his kitchen. On the table were an enormous box of lemons and packets of sugar stacked up in a towering pyramid. I stared in shock. There was so much sugar that dentists everywhere would be very, very worried. Kai stood with his hands on his hips. "The weather is warm, the sun is shining and everyone will want to buy some delicious lemonade from the Refreshment Royalty!"

"So we're not the Lords of the Lawn any more?"

Kai waved a hand. "That's in the past. Once we make a bathtub load of lemonade and sell it, we'll be Refreshment Royalty and rolling in money. We'll set up a stall out the front of my place, and everyone in the neighbourhood will come running to buy some."

"Your parents are okay with this?" I asked, just to make sure.

"A busy stall, making the neighbours happy, keeping myself out of trouble? They love the idea!" cried Kai.

I picked up a lemon. It was heavy, which meant it was full of juice. "Where did you get these from?"

"At the market," Kai said smugly. "I got a good price because I bought the whole crate."

"And the sugar?"

"Same. It's cheaper to buy lots of it."

I wasn't sure Kai had really done the maths. Or even thought about the maths. "No, it's not," I said. "If you buy a lot, it costs more than if you buy a little."

Kai rolled his eyes. “Okay, okay. But you have to think big in this business. That’s how you get to be Refreshment Royalty.” He rubbed his hands together. “Let’s get started.”

“One thing before we dive in,” I said. “What recipe are we using?”

Kai made a rude noise. “Recipe? Who needs a recipe? Lemonade is lemons and sugar and water. Dad told me what to do, and it’s easy!”

Looking back, that’s when I should have realised trouble was heading our way.

Every now and then, Kai's dad poked his head in to make sure all was going smoothly. Kai got a sore thumb from giving him the thumbs up all the time.

It took us hours to squeeze the lemons and put the juice in the big pot Kai had on the stove. He used a jug to add water and then he picked up a packet of sugar. He looked at it and read the label. He shrugged, opened it and emptied half of it into the pot. Then he thought for a second or two, shrugged, and sprinkled a little bit more in. "That'll do," he said.

I handed Kai a big wooden spoon. “Are you sure?”

“Pretty much.” He very carefully turned the stove on and started stirring. “I’ll let the sugar dissolve, and then we can do a taste test.”

It took ages because there was lots of water, lemon juice and sugar in the pot. Kai stirred and stirred. “My arm is getting tired,” he complained.

“Here, give me the spoon,” I said, taking over.

Eventually, the sugar had dissolved into the lemony water. I peered into the steaming pot. Yep, all good. “Time for the taste test,” I said.

Kai opened a kitchen drawer and scrabbled around. “Bingo!” he exclaimed, as he held up a ladle. Carefully, he leaned over and scooped up some of our magical mix. He held it up to his lips and then jerked back. “Hot, hot, hot!” he said. “We have to let it cool a little. All expert lemonade makers know that.”

He used his hand to fan the ladle. He whistled a little. I rolled my eyes and started juicing the rest of the lemons.

A few minutes later, Kai nodded, lifted the ladle to his mouth and sipped. For a moment, he didn’t say anything. He just blinked. Then he screwed up his face so hard, it looked as if it was going to cave in. He made a high-pitched squeaking noise, which turned into a sort of alarmed hiss.

I grabbed him by the shoulders. "Are you all right, Kai? Have you been poisoned or something?"

Kai opened his mouth and something like "Aaaaakaaak!" came out. He shook his head once, then twice, very vigorously. He dropped the ladle in the sink and rubbed his cheeks with both hands.

He looked at me, his eyes wide open. "Sour!" he gasped. "So sour!"

He grabbed a glass from the shelf and ran some water into it. He drank it in three big gulps. Then he had another one, rinsing his mouth out as he went.

I handed him a packet of sugar. “Let’s do it carefully this time,” I suggested. “Scoop some sugar in, taste a little bit, and add some more if it needs it. Then we’ll count up how much sugar we’ve used and how many lemons, and we’ll have the perfect recipe for next time.”

Kai applauded. “Vikram, that sounds almost scientific. I like it.”

Chapter 7

Sales Success!

When our first batch of lemonade was ready, we left it to cool down and went out to the front of Kai's house to set up a stall. Kai's dad found us plenty of paper cups and a couple of large jugs.

When our lemonade stall was ready, Kai stood back and tapped his chin with a finger. "We need a sign," he said, and he rushed inside to make one.

That left me to carry the heavy pot of lemonade outside. It had cooled perfectly because I'd found lots of ice cubes in Kai's freezer and emptied them into it.

I had to admit it, Kai's sign was pretty good. He'd made it using some spare wood and paint from the garage, and he'd also printed up some flyers. "We can't just wait for the customers to find us," he said as he handed them to me. "We have to go out and advertise."

So while Kai sat behind the table and helped himself to a nice refreshing cup of lemonade, I trudged up and down the street, handing out flyers. I gave them to people working in gardens. I gave them to people walking their dogs. I gave them to kids on bikes. I gave them to everybody I saw, and on such a nice, sunny day, all of them were interested.

We could be onto something here, I thought.

When I got back to the stall, there was a line of people waiting to be served. Kai was relieved to see me, and with two of us dealing out the lemonade, we soon had lots of happy customers.

An hour or so later, we had run out of lemonade and had lots of cash in our shoebox. “Sorry,” Kai said to the people waiting. “You’ll have to come back tomorrow.”

We got lots of groans for that, but plenty of the people promised that they’d come back – and bring friends.

As we packed up, Kai whistled happily and occasionally did a little dance. “The Refreshment Royalty,” he said. “We’re here to make people happy, to spread the word about the delights of lemonade, and to make a little money.” He shook the shoebox. “Let’s count it inside.”

We spread the coins and notes out on the kitchen table. Kai counted the money while whistling a jaunty tune.

When he’d finished counting, he punched the air. “We’ve made nearly twenty dollars, just like that!” Then he spread his arms wide. “They say that making the first million is the hardest, and I say that we’re well on the way.”

I rolled my eyes. “Okay, Mr Megabucks. Let me count it.” I was more careful, or better at counting – one or the other. “Sixteen dollars,” I said.

Kai shrugged. “What’s a dollar or two here or there when you’re running a modern business like ours?”

"It's the difference between success and failure." I frowned. "And talking about things like that, how much did the lemons and the sugar cost?"

Kai scratched his head. "What do you mean?"

"We can't say we made twenty dollars, or even sixteen, without subtracting what the ingredients cost. And that's not counting our time and effort, either."

"Sure we can!" He pointed at the money. "Sixteen dollars, right there!"

I shook my head. "Kai, it doesn't work like that. How much did you pay for the lemons and sugar?"

"Twenty-two dollars," Kai mumbled. He glanced at me. "Okay, twenty-four. But that was thanks to my clever bargaining."

I groaned. "So, after all that effort, all that time making the lemonade and all my time trudging up and down the street, we went backwards by eight dollars."

Kai stared at the notes and coins. "Times are tough for small business. But wait until tomorrow; things will be better."

I wanted to pull my hair out. "Kai, the more lemonade we sell, the more broke we'll be. We're not making a profit."

Kai held up a finger. "But we *are* making lemonade!"

I crossed my arms on my chest. "Not any more!"

Chapter 8

The Music Masters

On Saturday, I met Kai on his doorstep. "This time for sure," he said, and he held out a battered old hat.

I stared at the horrible object in my hand. It looked as if Muffin and Puffin had used it for a tug of war, and then a hippopotamus had danced on it. "What is this?" I asked. "Are we going to go into business selling second-hand clothes that no one would ever want to buy?"

Kai smiled and shook his head, as if I was the silly one. "No, Vikram, my good friend. We're going to need this for people to put money into. We're going to entertain people in the street. We're going busking."

On the one hand, busking wasn't such a bad idea. In our part of town, buskers often set up outside the shopping centre, or near the post office, or near the aged care home.

The buskers were people from school, mostly, with their violins and clarinets and proper instruments like that. On the other hand, Kai and I didn't play violins, or clarinets, or anything so classy. I really wasn't sure that Kai had any musical talent at all. Oh, he could whistle, but it was never a proper tune or anything. His whistling went up and down, all over the place, and round and round in circles, but it never sounded like anything recognisable.

Still, lack of talent, skill or training never stopped Kai from trying something. You had to be impressed by that.

"Busking." I handed the hat back to him and wiped my hands on my shirt. "And how do you think we're going to do that?"

"We're going to do it so well that we'll be known as the Music Masters," Kai said, seriously.

I saw where this was going. "I know, with t-shirts and caps and an *MM* emblem and all that – but what about the actual music part?"

"We're going to do it with the magic of modern keyboards. You can play a keyboard, can't you? I've seen you do it."

"That was when we were five years old, Kai. And it was one of those baby keyboards, with coloured keys and glitter."

Kai waved my objections away. "Pick it up on the way, and make sure it has fresh batteries."

This wasn't looking good. "And how about you?" I asked him.

He pulled a harmonica out of his pocket. "We'll be the Music Masters, a keyboard and harmonica combo."

I groaned. "You can't play a harmonica. I've never heard you play one, at least."

Kai shrugged. "How hard can it be? You just blow and move your mouth back and forth. It's about as basic a musical instrument as can be." He looked thoughtful. "Except for a drum, I guess."

I held up a hand. "Do not even dream about getting a drum. I'm getting a headache just thinking about it."

"So harmonica and keyboard it is," Kai said. "Mum!" he shouted over his shoulder. "We're going to the shopping centre." He turned back to me. "You know, people are going to be lobbing handfuls of money into this hat."

I saw how this was going to go. I could stand there on the doorstep and argue for a few more hours, and then we would end up doing what Kai wanted anyway and it would turn into a disaster, or I could pick up the keyboard on the way and save myself all the effort of arguing.

"I'll have to sneak into my little sister's room to get the keyboard," I said to Kai.

He grinned. "Do that, and we're on our way to musical millions!"

Chapter 9

Tough Competition

When we got to the shopping centre, we stepped into Trouble City.

At the entrance, next to the fountain, was a trio of violin-playing girls from school. They had an open violin case at their feet with lots of money in it, which was an eye-opener, all right.

A small crowd had gathered, and everyone was tapping their feet or bobbing their heads along with the music, which was pretty good, I had to admit.

"Maybe we should've checked out the location first," I said to Kai.

Kai narrowed his eyes. "Maybe they'll let us take a turn."

The girls finished their number, and they saw us approaching. "We're going to take a short break," said one of them to the crowd, and I recognised her as Mia from our class. The other two were her best friends, Cleo and Laura.

They came over to us. “Don’t even think about it,” Mia said. “This is our spot.”

I tried to be reasonable. “I think the spot belongs to the shopping centre, not you.”

Cleo snorted. “You’re new to this game, aren’t you? You probably don’t even have a permit.”

“We need a permit?” I turned to Kai. “We need a permit.”

“Obviously,” he said, but I don’t think he’d even heard of a busking permit. “It’s coming. Not a problem. Today, we’re just scoping out the scene.”

Mia wasn’t convinced. “Sure you are. Anyway, we were here first; it’s our spot.”

"Yeah," added Laura.

"Don't you point that stick at me!" Kai said to her.

Laura rolled her eyes. "It's a violin bow, not a stick." She looked him up and down. "You don't know much about music, do you?"

Cleo pointed at the keyboard I had under my arm. "Is that a baby keyboard? The one with the coloured keys? That's so cute!"

I blushed and Kai hustled me away. "Come on, Vikram. It looks like the Music Masters aren't appreciated here."

We left. I think the girls must have seen something funny then, because they started laughing a lot. Probably a clown or something.

Kai and I walked around the shopping centre, but wherever we looked, a busker had staked out a spot. We saw someone with a clarinet, two teenagers with trumpets and an older guy with a keyboard who was actually pretty good and making people dance. There was even one young drummer at the back of the shopping centre near the entrance to the car park. He was really hammering those drums, and he grinned at us as we went by. He pointed a drumstick at me. "Baby keyboard! Cool!"

We hurried past, and the echoes of his drumbeat followed us.

Kai grabbed my arm, and we stopped dead. "I've thought of the perfect spot," he said. "Quick, this way!"

Not far from the shopping centre was the local aged care home, where we'd visited Kai's Grandpa Stav a few times. It was a low brick building and had a lovely garden with a large flower bed out the front. "Old people love music," Kai said. "Grandpa Stav says it soothes their souls and reminds them of their younger days."

"Maybe it does, but where are we going to get some music like that?"

"Vikram, have faith in your ability," Kai said. "If we set up out here in the garden and lay down a few gentle tunes, they're sure to come out and ask us inside." He rubbed his hands together. "And old people can be very generous. Grandpa Stav gives the best birthday presents."

I took the keyboard out from under my arm. It was so brightly coloured, I really needed sunglasses, and it had a picture of a very smiley panda on it. "I haven't played this thing in years."

"You're a natural, Vikram. It'll all come back to you."

I grimaced. "All I can remember is 'Happy Birthday'."

"That's wonderful! Happy, bright, full of good celebratory feelings – it's perfect!"

"It's not my birthday. Or yours."

"Come on! It's bound to be someone's birthday! Play, Vikram! Play!"

I hesitated. "Why don't you give the harmonica a try first?" I asked him.

Kai whipped it out of his pocket. "What a good idea."

Kai took a breath, put the harmonica to his mouth and blew. A sick and weedy warble came out. Kai took it away from his mouth and frowned at it. "There must be something wrong with this thing. Maybe I shouldn't have kept it in that box of sawdust."

He shook his head and took in a mighty breath, so huge that his face went red. He put the harmonica to his mouth and blew as hard as he could. The harmonica bleated another sickly little sound, something like a seal with a stomach ache.

Right at that moment, Kai's Aunty Roula walked out of the aged care home with Clarence the goat on the end of a rope. She waved to Kai and me. "I was just visiting Grandpa Stav," she said. At the same moment, a tiny, feeble bleat came from Kai's harmonica. Clarence's head swung around. His eyes narrowed. He snorted and scraped at the ground with a hoof.

Kai waved. "Hi, Aunty Roula! Hi, Clarence! Listen to this!"

"No!" Aunty Roula shouted. "Clarence thinks it's an enemy goat! Stop!"

Too late. Kai gave the harmonica another colossal blow and another pathetic bleat emerged.

Clarence was enraged. He reared and tore the rope out of Aunty Roula's hand. He charged.

And that's how Kai and I got chased by an angry Clarence because he thought Kai was a rival goat. Aunty Roula ran behind us all, trying to catch Clarence and stop him from butting us into the next suburb. We raced around and around that flower bed a million times or more, until eventually we were red in the face, wobbly at the knees and totally out of breath. Luckily, so was Clarence. Not red in the face so much as wheezing like an old-fashioned steam train.

Clarence stopped and sat on his hindquarters. When he started eating the flowers, Aunty Roula caught up and grabbed the end of the rope. Then she put her hands on her knees and sucked in huge breaths of air. "Clarence," she gasped, and then she gave him a cuddle. "You're a naughty goat!" She turned to us. We were flat out on the ground, groaning. "He's the jealous type," she explained. "If he thinks there's another goat around trying to muscle in on his territory, he tries to do something about it."

Kai pushed back his sweaty hair. "Clarence thinks my harmonica playing sounds like a goat?"

I shrugged. "He might be a goat, but he's got a good ear."

Chapter 10

It Made a Great Story

Kai gave up. He talked to his parents and agreed that his pocket money could be suspended for a year to pay off the broken window. His parents thought that this was a lesson worth learning.

Kai was crushed – not just by the amount of money he wouldn't have, but because of the failure of his Big Ideas. One after the other, they had fallen over like dominoes.

A couple of months after this great series of disasters, I went around to Kai's place. I found him in the garage, where he was sorting through some old bicycle parts. "I got these for free," he explained when he saw me enter. "I thought I could put them together and make a couple of bicycles to sell, but I think they're too old and rusty for that." Then he sighed, "I probably shouldn't have even tried."

"You have to keep trying," I encouraged. "I get some good stories that way."

"What do you mean?" he asked.

I handed him a letter. "Read this."

I watched as he frowned over the paper. Then his eyes widened, and he began to grin. "You won a writing competition?"

"Sure did. And the prize will cover that broken window, with some left over."

Kai looked pained. "You don't have to pay for that window. It was my fault."

I took back the document. "I told you," I replied. "If I hadn't shifted the ladder, the basketball wouldn't have dropped onto the birdbath and then gone through the glass. Besides, what are best friends for?"

"What sort of story was it?" Kai asked, as he got to his feet. "A rip-roaring spy saga? A science fiction time-travel extravaganza?"

I smiled modestly. "Oh, it was a series of humorous adventures about two best friends trying to make some money and failing badly."

"Ah! A real-life tale!"

"More or less. It made for a great story, anyway."

Kai slapped me on the back. "Nice one, Vikram! We inspire each other, don't we?"

"Absolutely."

Kai scratched his head. "You said there was some money left over? What about two Hawaiian shirts? That won't break the bank."

"You want two Hawaiian shirts, now?"

Kai grinned. "One for me and one for you. And after we get them, we could make some extra money by washing cars in our new Hawaiian shirts!"

"I guess you're talking about Custom Coolest Carwashes?"

"The *CCC*? Vikram, you have the best ideas!"